WHO
Says
MOO?

For my dearest Lucy
—R. Y.

For Caitlin, Peter,
Halsey & Elizabeth
—L.C.E.

WHO SAYS MOO?

By Ruth Young

Illustrated by Lisa Campbell Ernst

Viking

Who says
moo?

Who says
squeak?

Who has
feathers
and a beak?

Who
looks up?

Who looks
down?

Who is
pink?

Who is
brown?

Who is
fuzzy?

Who says
quack?

Who has two bumps

on his back?

Who runs
fast?

Who goes
slow?

Who can
hold on
by her toe?

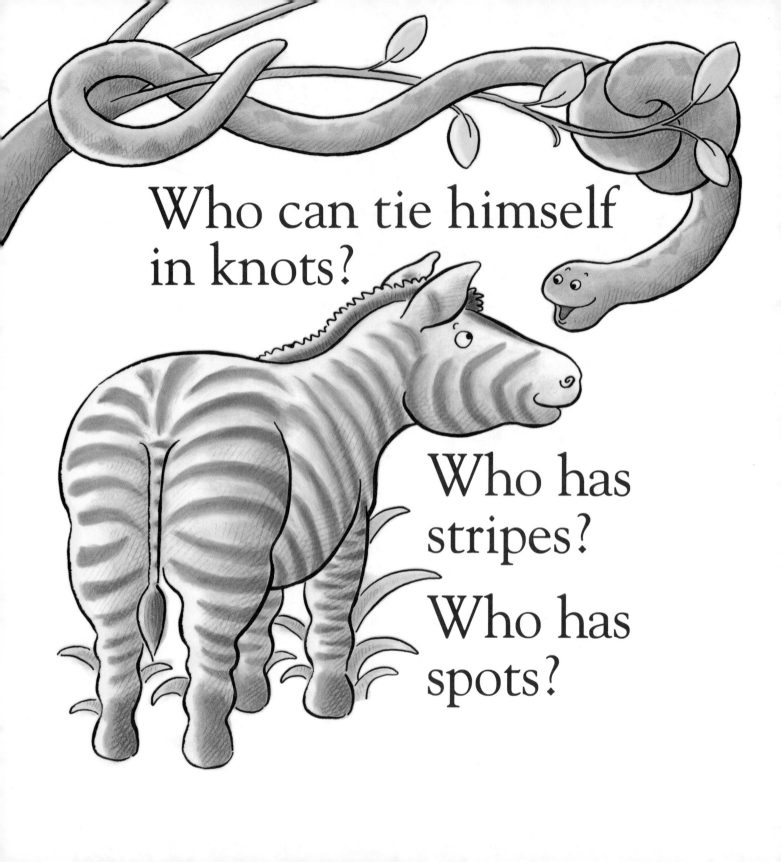

Who can tie himself in knots?

Who has stripes?

Who has spots?

Who thinks
mud's the place
for fun?

Who has
long ears?

Who has
none?

Who likes
water?

Who likes snow?

Who can swim and dive and blow?

Who stays
by the pond
and sings?

Who flies
through
the night
with wings?

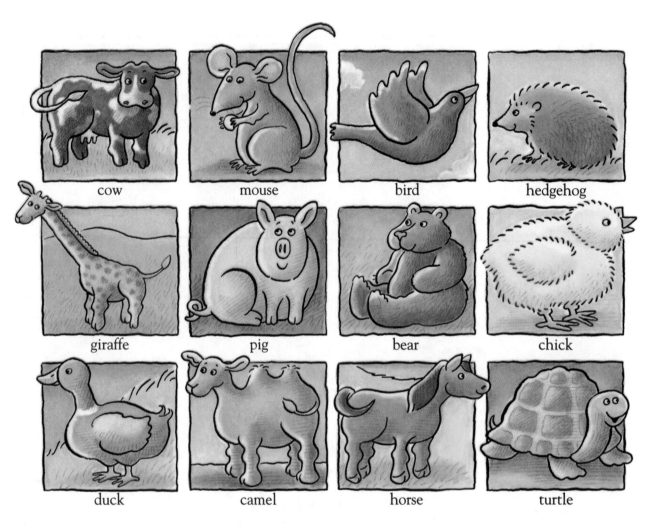

cow   mouse   bird   hedgehog

giraffe   pig   bear   chick

duck   camel   horse   turtle

Can you tell me who is who?

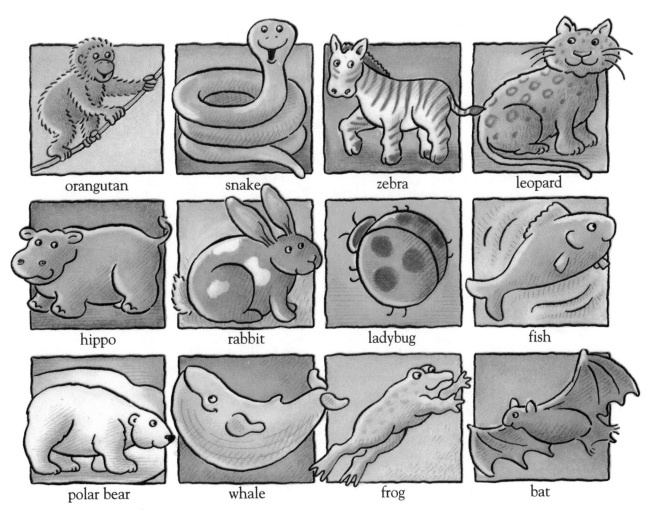

orangutan

snake

zebra

leopard

hippo

rabbit

ladybug

fish

polar bear

whale

frog

bat

Is there someone here like you?

VIKING
Published by the Penguin Group
Penguin Books USA Inc., 375 Hudson Street, New York, New York 10014, U.S.A.
Penguin Books Ltd, 27 Wrights Lane, London W8 5TZ, England
Penguin Books Australia Ltd, Ringwood, Victoria, Australia
Penguin Books Canada Ltd, 10 Alcorn Avenue, Toronto, Ontario, Canada M4V 3B2
Penguin Books (N.Z.) Ltd, 182–190 Wairau Road, Auckland 10, New Zealand

Penguin Books Ltd, Registered Offices: Harmondsworth, Middlesex, England

First published in 1994 by Viking, a division of Penguin Books USA Inc.

3   5   7   9   10   8   6   4   2

Text copyright © Ruth Young, 1994
Illustrations copyright © Lisa Campbell Ernst, 1994
All rights reserved

LIBRARY OF CONGRESS CATALOGING-IN-PUBLICATION DATA
Young, Ruth
Who says moo? / by Ruth Young ; illustrated by Lisa Campbell Ernst.   p.   cm.
ISBN 0-670-85162-0
1. Animals—Miscellanea—Juvenile literature.   [1. Animals—
Miscellanea.   2. Questions and answers.]   I. Ernst, Lisa Campbell, ill.   II. Title.
QL49.Y68 1994   591—dc20   [591]   94-11878   CIP   AC

Set in Goudy Old Style

Reprinted by arrangement with Viking, a division of Penguin Books USA Inc.
Printed in the USA.